TWISTED

THE VIDEOMANIAC

Wil Mara

An imprint of Enslow Publishing

WEST **44** BOOKS™

THE VIDEOMANIAC
HOUSE OF A MILLION ROOMS
THE TIME TRAP

WHERE DID MY FAMILY GO?
THE GIRL WHO GREW NASTY THINGS

Please visit our website, www.west44books.com. For a free color catalog of all our high-quality books, call toll free 1-800-542-2595 or fax 1-877-542-2596.

Cataloging-in-Publication Data

Names: Mara, Wil.
Title: The videomaniac / Wil Mara.
Description: New York : West 44, 2019. | Series: Twisted
Identifiers: ISBN 9781538383629 (pbk.) | ISBN 9781538383575 (library bound) | ISBN 9781538383520 (ebook)
Subjects: LCSH: Video games--Juvenile fiction. | Supernatural--Juvenile fiction. | Football--Juvenile fiction.
Classification: LCC PZ7.M373 Vi 2019 | DDC [E]--dc23

Published in 2019 by
Enslow Publishing LLC
101 West 23rd Street, Suite #240
New York, NY 10011

Editor: Caitie McAneney
Designer: Rachel Rising

Photo Credits: Cover (background) pixelparticle/Shutterstock.com; Cover (football screen) EFKS/Shutterstock.com; Cover (teen) Di Studio/Shutterstock.com; Back Cover STILLFX/Shutterstock.com.

Printed in the United States of America

CPSIA compliance information: Batch #CS18W44: For further information contact
Enslow Publishing LLC, New York, New York at 1-800-542-2595.

TWISTED

For Roger, with tremendous appreciation and gratitude.

The town of Kennisek held a flea market twice a year: once in the spring and once in the fall. To Brian Hart, it meant just one thing—*video game stuff.* No one around liked video games more than Brian. No one had a cooler collection. No one was better at playing them.

Brian and Elijah started at the first table. They looked over everything carefully. Then they went to the next table. Brian wanted to do it slowly. Elijah went along because that's what best friends did.

"Whoa," Brian said. "Hang on . . ."

The fourth table was mostly covered with junk. There were plates, dirty silverware, and an old toaster. But he saw a box tucked underneath. **"MISCELLANEOUS"** was written in marker across the front. There were all sorts of things inside: toy cars, pool balls, some broken jewelry, and a couple of Christmas ornaments.

Brian didn't really think there would be any video game stuff here. But he kept digging anyway. Two years ago, he'd found a Nintendo Game Boy at this very flea market. It was at the bottom of a box of old sheets and blankets. He realized then that he should always look. You just never knew. This time though, he found nothing.

Halfway down the second row, Brian saw a PlayStation 4 with a bunch of games. *First released in 2013*, he thought. He didn't mind older games. But the salesman said he wouldn't take it back if it didn't work. Brian wasn't willing to chance it.

In the third row, he found an old Mario Kart poster. Mario Kart was one of his favorite games. He talked the seller down to three bucks. But by the time they reached the end of the last row, he'd found nothing else.

"One poster," he said. "One lousy poster. And I have to wait six months until the *next* flea market!"

"Maybe some of the car people will have stuff," Elijah said.

The car people were sellers who came too late to get a table. They sold things out of their cars instead. They were always in the back of the lot.

"I doubt it," Brian said, "but I'll check it out . . ."

Elijah said he was going to go back to a table they had passed. It had kitchen stuff and he wanted something for his mom. Brian nodded and walked away. He was still whining under his breath.

The first car person had a bunch of wooden signs. He had carved and painted them himself.

3

The second car had the biggest collection of sunglasses Brian had ever seen.

The next few spaces were empty. Then Brian came to the very last spot. An old station wagon was parked in the farthest corner of the lot. Its back door was open. The seller's table was covered with all sorts of computer junk—monitors, keyboards, cables, and disc drives. But it wasn't the computer stuff that caught Brian's attention. It was the person selling it.

The man looked about a hundred years old.
He was thin and bony. A stubbly beard grew on
his saggy cheeks. Wispy white hair blew around
his bony head. He smiled at Brian. His teeth were
as yellow as old piano keys. And his eyes were the
darkest green Brian had ever seen. Like two perfect
gems.

Creepy, Brian thought. *Really creepy.*

"Good afternoon, my young friend," the
man said. His voice was deep and powerful.

"Umm, yeah . . . good afternoon."

"Allow me to introduce myself. I am Mr.
Odium, at your service. And you are . . . ?"

"I'm Brian."

"It is nice to make your acquaintance."

"Sure, you too."

Odium spread his hands out like a showman in a circus.

"Are you admiring my wares?"

"Your what?"

"My *wares*. That is the term for the things a humble vendor, such as myself, would sell to an interested buyer. Such as yourself."

Brian could feel his brain spinning. He tried to keep up with the man's strange speech.

"Umm, yeah . . ." he said again. "Sure."

"Of course you are. You are a wise young man. I can always spot a sharp mind at work!"

"Thanks," Brian said with a laugh. This guy must've spent some time in a nuthouse.

"You are welcome! And what might I have that would interest you today? Blessed, as you are, with the gift of youth, you are likely knowledgeable of the joys of technology, yes?"

Brian nodded. He was already back to

thinking about the Question of the Day—*Is there any gaming stuff?*

"I'm pretty good with computers, yeah," he said as he started looking through the piles. "But I'm really interested in video games."

"Ah!" Odium said. "A gamesman!"

Brian laughed again. "I like them a lot. Doesn't matter if they're action, role-playing, sports, whatever."

"Some parents don't approve of such things. But they can be very good for the mind." Odium tapped the side of his head.

"That's true," Brian said.

"And do you think you'll find something of value among the many treasures I've brought here today?"

Brian was hoping the guy wouldn't ask this. All the computer stuff he had was just too old. Most of it seemed to be from the 1980s and 1990s.

"I . . . I don't think so," he said carefully.

"I'm sorry. I don't see anything I can use here."

"Wait, wait!" Odium turned back to his station wagon and took out another box. "I have some things you might like. Some games!"

"Umm, okay . . ."

"I have *Crash Bandicoot,*" he said, walking through the CDs in the box with his fingers.

"No thanks," Brian said. *I think my dad used to play that.*

"*NBA Jam?*"

"No, sorry."

"*Quake?*"

"Nope."

"What about *Mortal Kombat?*"

"That's from, like, 1992," Brian said more angrily than he meant to.

Odium looked up from the box. A smile spread across his face. It showed off every one of his horrible mummy teeth. Even worse, Brian thought he saw Odium's green eyes *swirling* for just a moment. Like the color was liquid churning around and around.

"Ah, you're looking for something modern!" Odium said. "Something *new*!"

"Well . . . yeah, sure."

"I have just the thing for you, Master Brian." He held up one bony finger. "I ask for your patience, please."

He dug through the back of the station wagon again. This time he came out with a CD in a plain envelope.

"I believe," he said, "you will find this very much to your liking."

As Brian took it, their fingers touched. Odium's were freezing even though it was a warm day. And the skin didn't feel real, either. It didn't feel *alive*. It was more like the hard leather of an old baseball mitt.

Brian couldn't stop himself from pulling away. Odium didn't seem to mind, though. He just kept on smiling.

"Take a look," he said, "please."

Brian pulled the CD out of the little envelope. One side of it was shiny. That was the side the computer would read. The other side had two words in a scrawled handwriting—

ULTIMATE FOOTBALL

"What's this?" Brain asked.

"Is that not obvious?" Odium said. "It's a football video game. The *ultimate* football game, just as it says there. It has amazing graphics and sound. Also, it has unbelievable gameplay. And it's very easy to use!"

"I've never heard of it."

"No one has. You, my young friend, are the very first!"

Now Brian smiled back at him. "You made this?"

"I did indeed."

"You *programmed* this? Wrote the code and everything?"

The old man nodded. "That is correct, my friend."

Brian looked over the piles of out-of-date computer junk. Then he shook his head. He couldn't think of a thing to say.

"Before you decide my game is not worth your time," Odium went on, "I ask that you at least give it a try. If you still don't like it, then that's that."

Brian laughed and looked at the disc again. "Well, okay. I guess I've got nothing to lose. Wait, hang on. How much do you want for it?"

"Let's not discuss price just yet," Odium said. "I want all my customers to walk away happy. So as I say, go home and try it first. We will consider it a kind of test. And if you think it's good, then we can decide the price next time I see you."

"You mean six months from now? In the spring?"

"Yes. Does that sound fair?"

Brian shrugged. "Sure."

"Good, then we are in accord."

"Right—we are in accord." Brian didn't even know what "accord" meant.

Odium leaned his head back and laughed. Brian thought again that he was one of the weirdest people he'd ever met. Then he heard his name being called. He turned and saw Elijah waving at him from the tables.

"I have to get going," Brian said. "But thanks for this. I'll try it out as soon as I get home."

"I hope you enjoy it," Odium replied. Then he bowed grandly. "It was a very great pleasure to meet you today."

"Uh, thanks . . . you too."

"Hey," Brian said as soon as he caught up to Elijah. "What's going on?"

Elijah held up a bag. "I found an oven mitt for my mom. The one she has now is falling apart."

"Cool."

"How about you? Did you see anything?"

Brian showed him the CD. "This. It's supposed to be a football game."

"What do you mean, 'supposed to be'?"

"It's homemade." He pointed over his shoulder with his thumb. "By the creepy guy way in the back there."

Elijah looked at Odium over Brian's shoulder. "Wow . . . he looks weird."

"Tell me about it."

"You and your video games."

"You like them, too," Brian pointed out.

"Not as much as you do."

"*No one* likes them as much as I do."

Elijah laughed. "That's probably true. So do you know if this one even works?"

"No, but I'll give it a try later. I have to stop at the hardware store for my dad first."

"Okay, then let's hit the road," Elijah said.

Brian nodded. "Right."

As soon as Brian got home, he tossed the Mario Kart poster on his bed. Then he went to his computer. He put the CD in and waited. A little green light came on.

Then the screen went blank.

"Oh great, a virus!" he said angrily. *The old man's probably done this a million times. One of those computer hackers who just likes to bother people.*

He reached over to turn the computer off again. He prayed there'd still be something left of his hard drive when he turned it back on.

Then the following words came on the screen—

WELCOME TO
ULTIMATE FOOTBALL

A moment later, a second message replaced the first one—

PROPERTY OF:

MR. BRIAN DOUGLAS HART
325 OAK RIDGE LANE
KENNISEK, NEW JERSEY
07442

"Whoa . . ."

That message disappeared too, followed by—

ARE YOU READY TO PLAY?

Brian didn't type in his answer right away. He was trying to figure out how Odium knew his full name and address.

Maybe the program searched through my computer. Yeah . . . that must be it, he told himself. That information had to be somewhere in the computer's system. *Makes perfect sense.*

He tapped the "Y" key and waited.

The next message was—

CHOOSE AN OPTION:

1 **PLAYER VS. PLAYER**
2 **PLAYER VS. COMPUTER**
3 **COMPUTER VS. COMPUTER**

"Seriously? I can watch the computer play against itself?"

That was actually pretty cool, he had to admit. *I've never seen that before.*

He hit "3."

GOOD CHOICE, MY YOUNG FRIEND. NOW DECIDE WHICH GAME YOU WISH TO WATCH:

A list of sixteen possible games appeared. Brian picked number six—the New York Giants vs. the Washington Redskins.

VERY GOOD. AND NOW, PREPARE YOURSELF FOR ULTIMATE FOOTBALL . . .

This final message disappeared. The screen stayed blank for a few seconds. The little green light on the CD drive was still blinking. Something was happening.

Then came the sound of cheering. It was very weak at first—*GI-ANTS! GI-ANTS! GI-ANTS!*

As it grew louder, a picture began to form from the darkness. As it became clearer, Brian realized everything Odium had said was true.

The view was from high up. Like in a helicopter flying around the stadium. You could see everything—the fans, the players, and the cars in the parking lot. It was one of those opening shots you saw on TV. And that was exactly how it looked—like on TV. It was that real.

"Oh wow . . ."

A score appeared along the bottom—Giants 0, Redskins 0. The game hadn't started yet.

Then came the voices—

"Good afternoon and welcome to MetLife Stadium in New Jersey! I'm Robert Simmons along with Bobby Young, bringing you today's game. The New York Giants will battle their division rivals, the Washington Redskins, in week five of the NFL season."

"That's Simmons's voice exactly," Brian said to the screen. "*Exactly*. How is that possible?"

The camera view changed to the side of the field. Each team had their kickoff units in place. The Giants' kicker had his finger in the air.

"And we're just about ready," Young said. "Here we go . . ."

The kicker ran forward. He booted the ball high and hard. It sailed over the return man's head. Then it bounced out of the end zone for a touchback. The crowd cheered as the special teams players jogged off.

Brian watched the game in shock for the next three hours. The Giants beat the Redskins 12–6. Brian also discovered a few features to the game that Odium hadn't even told him about.

There were commercials, a halftime show, and after-the-game interviews. All the players were the same as those on actual teams right now. It was as if Odium had created his program yesterday.

When it was over, the picture and sound faded away. Then one last message appeared—

DO YOU WANT TO PLAY AGAIN?

This time Brian hit "N." The screen returned to the Windows desktop.

Brian was still in shock the next day. But
at least it was Sunday. That meant real football
games.

Elijah came over at 12:30, like always.

"Here," he said to Elijah, who was sitting
on one of the living room chairs. "One can of
Dr. Pepper, and one bag of Munchos." He tossed
the can first. Elijah caught it with both hands. He
didn't bother catching the bag of chips. He just let
them land in his lap.

"Thanks."

"I wouldn't open that can just yet," Brian
told him.

"Why not?"

"I dropped it when I took it out of the

fridge."

Elijah made a face and set the can down. "Good job, genius."

"I know."

"Speaking of genius, remember we have to do our report on Ben Franklin after this."

Brian nodded. "Right."

"Keep our perfect grades going."

"Right."

"And then we can—"

"Elijah?"

"Yes?"

"Shut up."

Elijah nodded. "Right."

A logo for the National Football League appeared on the giant TV screen. Then a deep voice said, "This is the NFL on CBS."

Brian turned the sound up. "Okay, here we go."

The screen went blank. Then the picture started coming in. Brian was lifting his soda to his mouth.

Then he stopped.

GI-ANTS, GI-ANTS, GI-ANTS...

"No," he said. His throat became very dry. "No way . . ."

Elijah looked over at him. "What's wrong?"

The camera showed the stadium from high up—like in a helicopter. The parking lot was loaded with cars. The autumn sky was blue and clear.

Then the voice of Robert Simmons—"Good afternoon and welcome to MetLife Stadium in New Jersey! I'm Robert Simmons along with Bobby Young, bringing you today's game. The New York Giants will battle their division rivals, the Washington Redskins, in week five of the NFL season."

Brian's face turned the color of old cheese.

"Bri, you okay?"

"I . . . I can't believe it."

"What?"

"It's exactly the same."

"What?"

"*Exactly* the same."

"What is?"

Brian pointed. "The game, the people, the players . . . everything. It's all the same!"

"I don't understand. Same as what?"

Brian pointed. "The Giants will kick off. Then the ball will go out of the end zone for a touchback. Watch . . ."

Elijah turned to see the Giants' kicker jog forward. He booted the ball over the head of the Redskins' return man. It then took a high bounce out of the end zone.

"So what?" Elijah said. "Touchbacks happen

all the time."

"No, keep watching. On the first play, the Redskins' quarterback will take a five-step drop. Then, against the Giants' blitz, he'll pass it to his tight end on the right side. The tight end will run eight yards. Then he'll be pushed out of bounds by Giants' safety Matt Clarke."

"What are you talking about?"

"*Watch* . . ."

Elijah turned back to the screen.

"Here's the first play of the game," the announcer said. "Looks like it's going to be a draw pl—. No, wait. Derek Mathison takes a five-step drop back for a pass . . . he's got time, but his main receiver isn't open. And now the pocket is breaking up . . ."

"He'd better hurry," the other announcer said.

"It looks like he'll have to . . . no, wait,

he's found an open man. It's Frank Barrett, his tight end on the right side. Barrett's got it . . . he's running . . . and he's pushed out of bounds by Matt Clarke. But not before a gain of about seven or eight yards. That's some heads-up offense by the Redskins."

Now Elijah's face had turned the color of old cheese, too.

"Uh, what's going on here?" he asked.

Brian kept watching for another moment. He already knew the next play. The Redskins were going to run the ball around the left side for a gain of only a yard. When this happened, he got up and started walking toward the stairs.

"Come with me," he said to Elijah. "You'll wanna see this."

They were back in the living room a few

hours later. The second game of the day was on—the Colts and the Chiefs. It was almost over.

"This is where Carlson fumbles," Brian said. On the screen, Chiefs' quarterback Bill Carlson took the snap. Then he dropped the ball as if it was covered in oil. He dove for it along with three Colts players.

"He gets it back, though," Brian added. "Remember?"

The referees dug through a pile of other players. Then Carlson jumped up with the ball in his hand.

Brian looked over to his best friend. Elijah was staring at the screen with his mouth hanging open.

"Now the Geico thing," Brian told him. A Starbucks commercial came on instead. "Oh no, that's right—Starbucks first, *then* Geico." Which is exactly what happened.

With eight seconds left in the game, Elijah finally spoke.

"The Chiefs punt it here," he said. "But the Colts' guy only runs it back to about the twenty-five. Then the game is over."

"Danny May punts it for the Chiefs," the announcer said. "A long, high spiral. Terence Phillips gets it at the nine for Indianapolis. It looks like he may have a hole . . . he's got some room to run. Wait . . . no. He gets taken down at the twenty-two as time runs out. And that wraps it up. Here at Arrowhead Stadium, the Chiefs have beaten the Colts twenty-four to ten. Stay tuned for the postgame show . . ."

Brian grabbed the remote and turned the TV off.

"Well?"

"It's . . . *unbelievable*."

"Yeah."

"And creepy, too," Elijah said. "Like really creepy."

Brian nodded. "No kidding."

Elijah thought quietly to himself for a moment. Then he said, "You need to get rid of it."

"I know."

"There's something . . . *not right* about it."

"I know. I don't even like having it in the house."

"Then chuck it."

"I'm gonna."

Elijah got up. "I've got to go. My mom's making burgers."

"Okay."

When they got to the front door, Elijah said, "Let me know when you get rid of that thing. I don't want to come back until it's gone."

Brian smiled. "I'm going upstairs to erase it from the computer right now."

"Good."

Brian went into Microsoft Windows and chose "Uninstall a Program." Then he clicked on Ultimate Football.

The following message appeared—

ARE YOU SURE YOU WANT TO REMOVE ULTIMATE FOOTBALL FROM YOUR SYSTEM?

Brian hit the "Y" key right away.

The next message was—

DO YOU REALLY THINK THAT'S A GOOD IDEA, BRIAN?

A chill went through his body.

"What the heck . . . ?"

He hit the "Y" key over and over.

YOU'RE SURE? ABSOLUTELY CERTAIN?

He tapped "Y" again. The screen finally went blank.

OKAY, THE FILES ARE BEING REMOVED FROM YOUR COMPUTER.

He let out a deep breath.

A bar on the screen started at 1%. Then it began moving slowly from left to right—2% . . . 3% . . . 4% . . . Below the bar was a button that said **CANCEL**.

Brian's cell phone made a ding sound. He had a new text message. He thought it would be Elijah. It was Cameron Peetey instead.

He rolled his eyes. In his group of friends, Cameron Peetey was the one who drove him nuts. Cameron's father was a lawyer or a banker or something. One of those jobs that made a lot of money. And Cameron loved to remind everyone how rich his family was. Brian couldn't care less. But it did bother him that Cameron had tons of video game stuff that he didn't.

Brian groaned and opened the message—

Dad got me another Xbox system today. It's the new one that came out last week. Didn't you want one of those?

Brian imagined smoke coming out of his ears. He reminded himself that beating other people with a hockey stick was against the law.

I'm really happy for you, Cameron. That's great.

He went to put the phone back in his pocket. Then it *dinged* again.

You can come over and look at it anytime, Cameron wrote.

"Yeah," Brian muttered. "I'll come over there and look at it. And then I'll jam it right—"

You can't play it, though, Cameron added a second later. Just look at it.

"Oh, you're just the worst, Peetey," Brian said.

He began typing a message back. It was the kind of message that would probably get him into trouble. But he didn't care.

Then he looked up at the computer screen and stopped typing.

He grabbed the mouse and clicked the **CANCEL** button over and over.

ARE YOU SURE YOU WANT TO STOP THE UNINSTALL?

He tapped the "Y" key like he was trying to kill a fly that had landed on it.

YOU ARE A VERY WISE YOUNG MAN, BRIAN. VERY WISE INDEED.

Another chill ran through him. But he couldn't worry about that right now. He went back to typing his text message.

I wouldn't dream of touching your new Xbox, Cameron. I think it's great that you got it.

He hit **SEND** and waited a moment. Then he typed some more—

So who do you think is going to win the football game Monday night?

On Tuesday, Brian sat down with the others in the school cafeteria. Everyone was there except Elijah, who had lunch at a different time. Brian gave them the biggest smile he could manage.

"Isn't it a great day?"

"It is if you're *you*," Lucas Robinson said. He set his chin into one brown hand.

Brian nodded. "Since I *am* me, I agree."

"Cameron is not happy."

"I know. Isn't it great? He didn't just lose. He lost *huge*." Brian pushed out the last word like a coyote howl—*huuuuge*. He loved saying this.

"How'd you do it?" asked Oliver Pitt. He was small, with messy hair and giant glasses. He was also the smartest kid in the school. It was like having Google for a friend.

Brian pretended to be innocent. He knew this question was coming.

"I, um . . . I have a formula," he said.

Emma Powell rolled her eyes. She was a smallish girl with short blonde hair.

"Oh please. You stink at math."

"I do not."

"Yeah you do," Oliver said.

"Well, okay, maybe. But it's still true."

"Then what is it?" Lucas asked. "What's your magic formula?"

Brian laughed. "I'm not going to tell you."

Cameron Peetey moved toward them like an elephant. He was by far the largest one in the group. He dropped into his seat with a thud. He and Brian stared at each other for a long moment. Then Cameron dropped a paper bag in front of him.

"There's your stinkin' *Call of Duty*," he said.

"Thaaaank you."

"I've never seen such luck in my life. How could you possibly guess the exact score of the game? The Dolphins haven't gotten over twenty-four points in one game all season."

"He has a *formula*," Emma said. Then she rolled her eyes again.

Cameron looked at Brian in disgust. "Seriously, that's what you expect us to believe?"

"It's true," Brian told him.

"You stink at math."

"I do n—"

The others looked at him with their eyebrows raised.

"Okay, fine. But I really did come up with a formula."

"And what is it?" Cameron asked.

"He won't tell us," Lucas said.

"Yeah, because he's lying," Cameron scowled. "It was luck, that's all. *Pure. Luck.*"

"No, not luck," Brian said. He made sure to keep that big, stupid grin on his face. "It's pure *genius*." He tapped the side of his head. Just like Odium had done.

"If that's true," Oliver said, "then do it again. Tell us what another score is going to be."

"Sure, name the game."

"The Steelers and the Bengals," Emma said. "This Thursday night."

Brian nodded. "And what are we betting?"

"You're serious? You're really going to bet stuff on this formula of yours?"

"Why not?"

Lucas smiled like someone who'd just won the lottery. "I want your *Destiny 2*!"

"Okay, and I want your new PlayStation

controllers," Brian told him.

"It's a bet."

"I want that old copy of *BioShock* you have," Emma said.

"No problem. And I want that new copy of *Monster Hunter* that you have."

"Done," she replied.

Brian looked to Oliver. "Well?"

"If you lose—which you will—I get your *Splatoon 2*," he said.

"And if I win, I get your *Uncharted: The Lost Legacy*."

"Okay."

Brian picked up the bag Cameron had thrown in front of him. "Wanna try to win this back?"

Cameron looked angry enough to punch a hole through a brick wall. "And if you get lucky again?"

"Your old Xbox system."

"What?!"

"You heard me."

"You're crazy," Cameron said in a nasty voice. "You know that?"

"But you're not using it anymore, remember? You got the new one now."

"Yeah, I know."

"Then make the bet," Brian said.

Another moment of deadly silence crept between them.

"Fine," Cameron said. "It's a bet."

"Excellent."

Brian whistled as he began unpacking his lunch.

He couldn't remember the last time he felt so excited.

Brian sat in his room watching the Steelers-Bengals game on the computer. The final play was a pass by the Bengals for eleven yards. But it didn't matter because the Steelers were ahead 31–9. The Bengals' defense had been sloppy all day. They never had a chance.

"This is awesome," Brian said to himself. He wanted to laugh but didn't. "Just *awesome*."

He reached for his cell phone. It was sitting on top of his history book. The report on Benjamin Franklin had been totally forgotten.

He'd already made space in his room for all the new stuff that was coming. Lucas's PlayStation controllers would look perfect on the shelf next to his T500 RS Force Racing Wheel. And the new games—Emma's *Monster Hunter* and Oliver's *Uncharted: The Lost Legacy*—would go on the shelf below that. Best of all was Cameron's old Xbox. Brian didn't have an Xbox because his parents would only buy him one gaming system. He'd chosen a PlayStation.

But now I'll have both, he told himself.

And this was just the beginning! As long he had Odium's football program, he could win so much stuff from the others. More games, more controllers, more collectibles. And someday . . . *wow* . . . someday . . .

Cameron's NEW Xbox system!

"That's right," he said, pumping his fist in the air. "It's gonna be all mine. And then I won't let *him* touch it!"

He went back to his phone and started typing—

Hi Guys. My formula tells me that the Steelers will beat the Bengals by more than 20 points. So I'm gonna say the score will be something like 31–9.

He was just about to hit **SEND**. Then he stopped.

No . . . wait . . . hang on a second here . . .

The stupidity of what he was about to do hit him like a punch in the face.

It all played out in his head like a movie. If he made this bet, the others would lose, of course. Then they'd give him all that stuff. But after that, they'd never make another bet with him. Why would they?

The first time he won could be explained as pure luck. Everyone got lucky sometimes. But to guess an exact score twice in a row . . . after saying you had some kind of formula . . .

That would prove that the formula *worked*!

And they'd never bet with him again. Then he'd never win anything else from them.

No more games, no more controllers, and no chance at Cameron's new Xbox . . .

He looked back down at the phone. The message was still there, waiting to go. And his thumb was hanging over the **SEND** button.

He pulled it away. He sat there thinking for a few moments.

He erased the message and typed a new one—

Hi guys. My formula tells me that the Bengals will beat the Steelers by just 3 points. And there won't be a high score. Both teams have such good defense. So I'm gonna say 17–14.

His heart was pounding. But he was smiling.

"Yeah," he said, "this is *perfect*."

He hit **SEND**.

"Hey, there he is!" Lucas called out as Brian walked to the cafeteria table the day after the game. "It's *Formula Guy!*"

"Ooo!" Emma slapped her hands to her cheeks. "Is it really you, Formula Guy?"

"Tell us who's going to win the Super Bowl, Formula Guy!" Oliver added. "And the World Series, too!"

Brian dropped into his seat. Then he put on his best mad-and-sad-at-the-same-time face.

"Shut up, all of you," he said.

"Wow, seventeen to fourteen," Lucas went on. There was so much joy in his voice. "Not even *close!*"

"You didn't even pick the right *winner*," Oliver pointed out.

"And I like that comment about the defenses being so good." Emma elbowed him and winked. "Nice job with that one, Formula Guy. You didn't just lose, y'know. As you love to say, you lost *HUUUGE*!"

"Okay, okay," Brian said sharply. "I screwed up, I got it." He shook his head. "I don't understand. It worked perfectly the first time."

"Luck," Oliver told him. "Just like Cameron said."

Brian slammed his hands on the table. "No, it wasn't luck! That formula works!"

"Well, duh," Emma said. "Clearly not."

"It *does*, believe me." Brian put his bag on the table. He started unpacking his lunch. "It does," he said again.

He unwrapped his sandwich—ham and

cheese—and took a bite. Then he noticed that the others were staring at him.

"What? You've made fun of me enough, haven't you?"

"We have," Emma said.

"But since you've brought your lunch—" Lucas began.

"—shouldn't you have brought something else, too?" Oliver finished.

They all put their hands out.

Brian rolled his eyes. He picked up his backpack from the floor. Digging through it, he handed each of them a game cartridge.

"Fine," he said. "I hope they cause all of your systems to crash. And then, I hope—"

"Well, well, well," said a new voice.

Brian took a deep breath and shook his head. Cameron Peetey was standing on the other side of the table. His arms were folded, and he had a huge smile on his face.

"Don't start with me, buttface," Brian said. He reached into his backpack again. Then he found the last game cartridge and slid it over. "There. There's your stupid game."

Cameron didn't seem to see it. He just sat down and leaned as close to Brian as he could.

"*Pure. Luck.*" he said. "Just like I thought."

"It was *not* luck," Brian shot back.

"Yeah it was." Cameron unzipped his little cooler bag.

"Of course it was luck the first time," Oliver said. "If you had a real formula for knowing the scores of sporting matches, you'd be a billionaire."

Brian made a fist and clenched his teeth. He wanted to look angrier than ever. But inside he was thinking, *This is going perfectly! It's like having four big fish biting on the same hook!* The hardest part was trying not to show how excited he felt.

"I'm telling you," he went on, "I really do have a formula."

"Yeah?" Lucas said. "Then how come you just gave us a bunch of your games?"

"Because I made a mistake with the formula last time."

"Oh, *riiight*," Emma said.

"I did—but I know what the mistake was, and I'm going to fix it."

"Of course you will," Oliver added.

Cameron said, "Give us a break, huh?"

Brian felt like he could explode with happiness. *I've almost got them . . . almost . . .*

"You think I'm wrong, Peetey boy?" he asked.

"I know so."

"No," Brian said. "*You are.*"

They stared at each other with something close to real hatred. *Here it comes*, Brian thought.

Any second now . . .

"Oh yeah?" Cameron said. "Then make another bet. *I dare you.*"

The other three joined in immediately—

"Yeah, come on Brian!"

"Whip out that formula of yours!"

"I'd love to win some more of your stuff!"

Meanwhile, one word was flashing through Brian's mind—*YES!!! YES!!! YES!!!*

"Umm—okay," he said. "What do you guys have in mind?"

One week later, Brian was sitting in his room playing Emma's *Minecraft*. He was also using Lucas's controllers. And he was wearing Oliver's headset. But most awesomely, it was all running through Cameron's old Xbox system.

All the other stuff he won was in a bag on the floor. This included a DualShock wireless controller, a bin for cartridges, a T-shirt that had **"I'D RATHER BE GAMING"** on the front, and a sign he planned to put outside his bedroom door. It read **"ALERT! VIDEO GAME IN PROGRESS!"**

"I seriously cannot believe you won again," he heard Oliver say through the headset.

"It's ridiculous," Lucas added.

Then Emma's voice—"Unbelievable."

"Hey, what can I tell you, guys?" Brian said with a smile. "When a formula works, it works. And this time it did. Which means I won, and you guys lost—"

"*HUUUUUGE*," the three of them said at the same time. Then Emma finished with, "Yeah, yeah. We know."

Cameron had been very quiet since they got online. Brian thought this was great. He wanted to say, *What's the matter, Peetey boy? Miss your Xbox?* He knew that would be really mean. So he didn't say it. But Cameron would definitely say something like that to him.

"Oh *please*," Oliver said. "You lost all those other bets before you finally won again. How is that a good formula?"

"Exactly," Emma jumped in. "You won *twice* in fifteen bets. Big deal."

"If you won again," Lucas cut in, "maybe—
maybe—I could see that your formula was real.
But . . ."

"It isn't," Cameron finally said. It was
the same low, dangerous voice he'd used in the
cafeteria. It made Brian think of an angry bull,
scratching the dirt right before it charges at you.
"It's nothing but luck, like I've been telling you
guys all along."

Brian was just about to say, *Maybe you'd like
to try another bet?* But then the door opened. Elijah
walked in.

"Hey!" Elijah said.

Brian's smile dropped to a frown. He didn't
know Elijah was going to come over today.

"Uh . . . hey."

"My mom wants to know if you and your
parents want to come over for din—"

Elijah came to a dead stop. He was looking

at the bag of stuff on the floor. Then his eyes went to the controller Brian was holding. Then to the headset. Then to the Xbox.

"One sec, one sec!" Brian told him, putting a finger in the air. "I'm stepping away for a minute, guys," he said into the microphone. Then he muted it.

He took the headset off and put both hands up. "I know what you're going to say."

"Brian—"

"I know, it's bad."

"It's not just bad," Elijah said. "It's like *stealing*."

Brian nodded. "I know. I know it is. And I'm sorry."

"Not sorry enough!"

"Yes I am! In fact . . . in *fact* . . ." Brian's finger was still up. "I was planning to give everything back. All of it!"

Elijah crossed his arms. "Sure you were."

"I was, I swear. I *swear* it!"

"Then why haven't you?"

Brian grinned. "I just wanted them to suffer a little bit more before I did."

"Bri—"

Brian groaned. "Okay, *fine*. I'll give it all back this weekend. I just want to play with it all for a few more days."

"Tomorrow," Elijah said.

"This weekend."

"*Tomorrow.*"

"Friday. Just two more days. Come on, that's no big deal!"

Elijah rolled his eyes. "Fine, Friday."

"Sweet."

"And you said you were going to get rid of that creepy football game, too."

"Also on Friday. I promise," Brian told him.

"You can even come over and check."

"You better. I want you to erase it completely."

"I will, I swear."

"Okay."

"Okay." Brian patted him on the shoulder. Then he turned and grabbed a second headset and keyboard off the floor. "So, do you wanna get in the game with us? We're in survival mode!"

"We both have homework to do. The Ben Franklin report, remember?"

"We can work on it later."

Elijah looked at his watch. "It's already 4:30."

"So we'll do it after dinner. You were going to say we're invited to eat at your house, right?"

"Yeah."

"Okay, so there you go." Brian put the headset around Elijah's neck. Then he put the wireless controller in his hand. "We'll play now, have dinner, then do the report."

Elijah looked unsure.

"Dude, Cameron's hunger bar is down to almost nothing. You don't want to miss that, do you? It's probably the only time in his life he's gone this long without food!"

Elijah smiled and shook his head. "Sure, whatever."

"My *man*!" Brian put his own headset back on. Then he unmuted the mike.

"Okay, peeps, new player coming in!"

Brian went out to the garage on Thursday night. That's where his parents put cardboard boxes to be recycled. He found a big one and took it back to his room. Then he started packing up the things he'd won.

He set each piece into the box carefully. The headset, the controllers, the Xbox, the copy of *Minecraft*—he loved all of it. He loved how it looked, how it felt. And he never had this *much* before! Gaming stuff was so expensive. He didn't really have any money anyway. Sometimes he did chores around the house or cut Mr. Peterson's lawn next door. But none of that paid a lot. He was also too young to get a job. So he only got new game stuff on his birthday or some holiday.

He imagined having piles of it. Every game, every controller, every system . . . every *everything*. It would be ready to use whenever he felt like it. Everyone would think of him as some kind of video game king. No, even better—a *videomaniac*. He'd have the best collection of gaming stuff around!

Then Elijah blew this dream away. Brian kept hearing Elijah's voice in his head. *It's like stealing, Brian! It's just like stealing!* At first Brian tried to ignore it. Then he got tired of it. Now it was making him mad.

Once everything was packed in the box, he went to the computer. He had to remove the program. If he didn't, Elijah would bug him about *that*, too.

He went back to the "Uninstall a Program" menu. Just like last time, he had to answer a bunch

of questions first—

ARE YOU SURE YOU WANT TO REMOVE ULTIMATE FOOTBALL FROM YOUR SYSTEM?

He typed "Y."

Then—

DO YOU REALLY THINK THAT'S A GOOD IDEA, BRIAN?

He typed "Y" again.

YOU'RE SURE?
ABSOLUTELY CERTAIN?

He sighed and tapped the "Y" key one more time.

OKAY, THE FILES ARE BEING REMOVED FROM YOUR COMPUTER.

The same status bar appeared—2% . . . 3% . . . 4% . . . And there was the **CANCEL** button below it again. Brian really wanted to click on it.

When the uninstall reached 99%, the screen went blank.

"What the heck?!"

He waited another moment, but nothing happened. He started hitting different keys and clicking the mouse like crazy. He looked down at the computer's tower. The little light on the drive was flashing away.

Okay, so something is going on . . .

He lookcd back to the screen. A new

message was waiting for him—

IT ISN'T REALLY LIKE STEALING, BRIAN. YOU KNOW THAT, RIGHT?

"Huh?!"

COME ON NOW. THEY'VE ALL WON STUFF OFF YOU BEFORE. WHAT'S WRONG WITH YOU WINNING SOME STUFF OFF THEM?

Brian read this over a few times. Then he nodded.

"Yeah, that's true. They have."

Then a voice in Brian's mind said, *It really IS like stealing—and you know it.*

He knew this voice very well. He heard it all the time. It was the one that made him finish his homework as soon as he got home from school. Or help his dad clean out the garage without being asked. And tell his mom how nice she looked after she got a haircut.

You have a program that tells the scores of football games, Brian! the voice went on. *How is that fair to the others? How is that NOT stealing?!*

Then another message came on the screen—

BECAUSE IT'S JUSTICE, BRIAN.

"Justice?" he asked out loud.

THAT'S RIGHT. HAVEN'T THEY DONE SOME MEAN THINGS TO YOU? SOME REALLY MEAN THINGS?

"Well . . . yeah, a few things. Sure."

He started to remember. There was the

time Oliver let the air out of his bicycle tires. And the time Lucas beat him in one-on-one basketball and wouldn't shut up about it for days. Emma once pegged him in the back of the head with a snowball. She laughed so hard she almost passed out.

Then there was Cameron. Brian couldn't even list all the things Cameron had done to annoy him. *If I had a dollar for every snotty thing Cameron ever said . . . bragging about all the money he had to buy gaming stuff . . . then reminding me that I didn't have any . . .*

And what about Elijah? His *best friend* since forever. His best friend. Elijah was making him give all the stuff back. And erase the program. *Ordering* him to do it, like he was Brian's father or something.

THEY DON'T SOUND LIKE VERY GOOD FRIENDS TO ME, BRIAN.

"No," Brian said. "They don't."

He looked at Oliver's headset. It was sitting in the box on top of everything else. It was such a nice one. So much better than the one Brian had been using for the last three years. The sound wasn't as good. And sometimes the wireless connection cut out. But Oliver's headset . . .

NO, BRIAN.
IT'S YOUR HEADSET.

"That's right," Brian replied. "*My* headset—"

His headset was fantastic. The best one you could get.

The other voice in Brian's head tried to speak a few times—

You know they were only kidding when they did those things.

You know they didn't mean anything.

You know they consider you a real friend. Even Cameron, in his own weird way.

You know how hurt they'd be if they knew that you'd been . . .Been . . .

Been . . .

"What?" Brian asked. He was feeling really angry now. "Stealing?!"

NO, NOT STEALING. YOU KNOW WHAT IT IS. GO AHEAD AND SAY IT.

"It's *justice*!" Brian said. "I'm just getting them back for the mean things they've done!"

THAT'S RIGHT. DON'T LET ANYONE TELL YOU DIFFERENT.

"I won't. Not Lucas, not Emma . . ."

NOT EVEN ELIJAH?

"No." Brian shook his head. "Not even *him*."

GOOD. NOW, DO YOU REALLY
WANT TO ERASE THIS PROGRAM?

Brian reached for the "N" key. He waited for just another second—then hit it hard.

GREAT, BRIAN. NOW GO TAKE
YOUR STUFF BACK OUT OF THAT BOX.

"I will," he said.

There they are, Brian thought as he walked into the cafeteria. The four of them were sitting at the same table. *Perfect.*

He watched one of Sunday's games on the computer last night. It was the Dolphins and the Patriots. The scores for all the other games were at the bottom of the screen, too. His plan was to lose this week. That way they'd get all their stuff back. Then he would win next week. That's when he would get it all. He'd get Cameron's old Xbox *and* his new one. And Emma's set of wireless speakers. And Lucas's stand with a cooling fan. And Oliver's external 2TB expansion drive. He'd have *EVERYTHING*.

Thinking about it now made him feel happier than he'd ever been in his life.

"Yo!" he said as he sat down. He even gave Cameron a smile. "What's going on?"

"Not much," Emma said quietly. She was picking through her spaghetti but not eating it.

"No?" He looked around. "You guys don't seem very cheerful! It's Friday, y'know."

"Nothing to be cheerful about, I guess," Lucas said.

Brian's eyebrows popped up like a pair of pinball flippers. "No? Well, how about this—my formula tells me the Dolphins are going to beat the Patriots on Sunday. By *three touchdowns*."

In truth, Brian knew it was the Patriots who would win by three touchdowns. He planned to say he used the formula wrong and got the score backward. The others would laugh at him, of course. Then Brian would have to give them all their stuff back. After that, they'd be dying to make another bet.

Perfect, he thought again.

"That's nice," Oliver said. He wasn't really paying attention. He was playing some game on his phone.

Brian nodded. "I know, right? Crazy! But hey, that's what my formula is telling me. So, what I'm thinking of betting this time is—"

"There isn't going to be any betting," Cameron told him.

Brian's smile faded away. "What are you talking about?"

"No more bets," Cameron said.

He looked at the others. He could tell they had all talked about this before he got there.

"What do you mean? This is a great bet!"

"We don't care," Emma said. "We don't care if you think the Dolphins are going to win by a hundred touchdowns."

"*What?!*" Brian felt like he wanted to jump out of his skin.

"Our parents are pretty mad," Oliver said.

Lucas said, "My dad told me I'd be grounded for a week if I made another bet."

Emma said, "My mom said I'd be doing all the laundry in the house for a month."

Cameron added, "And both my parents want to know who I've been betting *with*." He pointed a chubby finger at Brian. "So far I've gotten away with not telling them. But if they keep asking . . . I'm gonna."

"But you guys can win all your stuff back!" Brian said. "I was going to bet everything you've lost so far! I mean, come on! It's the Dolphins and *three touchdowns* over the Patriots!"

They all shook their heads.

"Sorry," Cameron said, "but forget it."

Brian slapped his hand on the table. "You guys are *nuts*! You know that?"

Part of him couldn't believe he was acting this way. *These are your friends*, his Good Voice cried out. *What are you doing?!*

"Brian!" Lucas said, horrified. "Take it easy!"

"Yeah," Emma added. "Calm down!"

"I gave you guys a great bet!" Brian yelled. "And you won't take it? Some friends I've got!"

"*Brian*!" Cameron boomed. Now some of the other kids in the cafeteria turned to watch. "Get a hold of yours—"

"No!" Brian said. His voice was lower but still angry. He pointed at Cameron, then the rest of them. "Don't tell me to calm down! How dare you do this to me!"

He turned and stormed off. He was thinking about Odium's words on the screen—*They don't sound like very good friends to me, Brian.*

"They aren't," he said to himself. "Not at all."

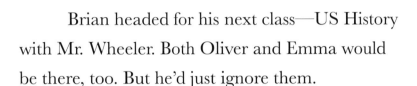

Brian headed for his next class—US History with Mr. Wheeler. Both Oliver and Emma would be there, too. But he'd just ignore them.

As he turned the first corner, he saw Billy Carson standing at his locker. Billy was on the school's basketball and baseball teams. But everyone knew his favorite sport was football.

A new plan came together quickly in Brian's head. When he reached Billy, he patted him on the shoulder. His anger was gone now.

"Hey there," Brian said cheerfully. "What's going on?"

Billy looked back to see who it was. "Oh,

hey! What's happening, Brian? I haven't seen you around in awhile."

"That's because we don't have any classes together this year. But I was watching the games last Sunday and thought about you."

"Oh man, wasn't that Denver game great?"

"It sure was," Brian said. He put on the biggest smile of his life. "So who do you think is going to win the Dolphins-Pats game this week?"

After dinner on Monday, Brian went to his room to play *Fortnite*. Elijah stormed in about a half hour later. He opened his mouth to say something. Then he froze when he saw what was in Brian's room.

There was gaming stuff *everywhere*.

In one corner was a pile of controllers. There were joysticks, gamepads, racing wheel-and-pedal combos, trackballs, and throttle quadrants. On the dresser stood six tall stacks of games in their cases. Elijah knew some of them very well—*The Legend of Zelda*, *Call of Duty*, and *Assassin's Creed*. Others he'd only heard of, like *Injustice* and *Persona*.

About ten miles of spare cables lay on the

floor. They were mostly USB and HDMI, tangled together like a nest of snakes. There were also a few gaming systems, including a PlayStation, Xbox, and Nintendo. They all looked like they were brand new.

"Oh my God . . ."

"Don't bother calling first or anything," Brian said. He never took his eyes away from the screen. His *Fortnite* character jumped on a horse and rode off.

"I did try to call you. About *twenty times*."

"Didn't hear it. Too busy."

"Yeah, I see that. I guess you didn't give back the stuff you won like you promised."

"Nope."

"And I guess that means the game is still on your computer."

"Yep."

"And I hear you're making bets with other

people now, too. Like Billy Carson and Andy Hall and Scott Evans."

"Yep."

"Bri, you need to stop this."

"Nope."

"It's not honest."

"It is to me."

"What?"

"I said, 'It is to me.'"

"How can you think that?"

"I have my reasons."

"Such as . . . ?"

Brian thought about explaining the whole "justice" thing. Then he decided Elijah wouldn't get it. People like Elijah never understood stuff like that.

That's something about Elijah that's always bugged me, Brian thought. *He's always trying to teach me what's right and what's wrong. It's like having a second father for a best friend. I've already got a father. I really don't need another one.*

"It's none of your business," Brian said finally. On the screen, a creeper and an enderman appeared. Brian killed both of them with his sword.

"What did you just say?" Elijah asked angrily.

"You heard me."

"Yeah, I did. But I can't believe it."

"Well, believe it. Now leave me alone, wouldja?"

Elijah looked mad enough to kick a car over. He turned to leave, then turned back. He stepped over one pile after another until he got to the flat-screen TV.

Confused, Brian said, "What are you d—"

Elijah yanked the power cord out of the wall. The *Fortnite* images disappeared and the screen went blank.

Brian jumped up. "What's the matter with you?!"

"Me?!" Elijah moved so close that their faces were inches apart. "What's the matter with *YOU?!*"

"There's nothing wrong wi—"

"You're going crazy with all this stuff! You're stealing from your friends! How do you not see that?!"

"It's *justice*, Elijah!" Brian yelled back. "How do *YOU* not see *THAT*?!"

Elijah stared at him in disbelief.

"Did you say 'justice'?"

Brian nodded. "Yeah . . . sure. Justice."

"For what?"

"For, y'know . . . all the bad stuff they've done to me."

Elijah's eyes widened. "What are you *talking* about?!"

"Well, like . . . like the time Emma hit me with that snowball."

"*WHAT*???"

"Yeah. Right on the back of the head. It really hurt, too!"

"That was an *accident*! And she still said she was sorry!"

"What about the time Lucas beat me in basketball? He wouldn't stop talking about it!"

A little smile came onto Elijah's face. "You can't be serious. He was kidding around. You know that." Before Brian had a chance to say anything back, Elijah kept going. "And Billy Carson? What has he ever done to you? Or Andy, or Scott? You hardly know those guys. So why are they being cheated by you?"

"Well . . . I'm sure . . . I'll bet that someday they might. . ."

"And what about me? If I hadn't known

about that program, would you have tried to cheat *me*, too?"

A long silence came between them. It was like the calm in the middle of a hurricane. Brian wanted to give him an answer. But they had known each other too long for him to get away with a lie.

Elijah started nodding. The hurt came over his face like a cloud blocking the sun.

"Okay, I understand. Your video games are more important than everything else. More important than your family. More important than your grades. And more important than your friends. Even your best friend. Isn't that right?"

Elijah waited for an answer, but none came.

Shaking his head, Elijah said, "See you around, Bri."

He turned and walked out.

One Month Later

There were five characters on Brian's television—a female Fighter, a male Fighter, a Mage, an Assassin, and a Marksman. They were fighting their way to the enemy's Tower. It was one of the best battles Brian had ever seen in *League of Legends*. The goal was to destroy the enemy's Nexus. And they'd do it, too. He knew how good the five players behind those characters were.

Emma was the female Fighter. Oliver was the male Fighter. Lucas was the Mage. Cameron was the Assassin. And Elijah was the Marksman.

And Brian would've given anything to be part of it.

He'd been blocked by all five of them. And not just on League of Legends but all online games. He sent them messages begging them to unblock him. But they ignored him. Same with his texts, his calls, and his emails. He didn't even sit with them in the cafeteria anymore. The last time he tried, they wouldn't talk until he left. Now he ate at a table by himself.

He tried joining some other online teams. But it just wasn't as much fun. He couldn't call anyone a butthead. He couldn't tell them their last move was bad. He couldn't say their character looked stupid. A few days ago, he was playing *Counter-Strike: Global Offensive* with a kid from Michigan. At one point the kid missed an easy shot at a Counter-Terrorist. Brian told him he was an idiot who should put his glasses back on. He got kicked off that team about three seconds later.

He looked through all his games for one he

could play by himself. He didn't really like games that you played alone. There was *Horizon Zero Dawn* for the PlayStation. There was *Rise of the Tomb Raider* for the Xbox. He also had *Prey* and *Fallout*. Those last two were maybes. He hated most of the others.

So why did I bother trying to win them?

He kept looking through the pile. Then something caught his attention. It was a photo on his dresser. It showed Brian and his friends when they went whitewater rafting last summer. They were all wearing shorts, T-shirts, and orange floater vests. They were standing in front of their raft holding their oars in the air. Everyone was soaking wet. Oliver had fallen into the water twice. Lucas had fallen once. Brian almost fell in, too. *But Cameron grabbed my hand*, he remembered. *Then he and Elijah pulled me back*. That was one of the best days of his life. One of those days when your face hurt because you'd been laughing so much.

The stacks of games had been blocking the picture. Looking at it now, he felt a wave of sadness. Then his anger sort of wiped it away.

Those same people are pretending you're not even alive anymore.

He took a deep breath. Then he got the remote from the floor and turned off the television. He couldn't even remember the last time it had been off.

He headed for the door. His plan was to get a bowl of cereal in the kitchen.

Then a message appeared on his computer screen—

WHAT'S WRONG, BRIAN? HOW COME YOU'RE NOT PLAYING?

"Huh?" he said. "How did that get there?" He thought he had put the computer into sleep mode.

He dropped into the chair in front of it.

"Those guys won't let me play anything with them," he said.

I'M SORRY TO HEAR THAT.

"They won't talk to me. They won't text me. Nothing."

**I TOLD YOU THEY
WEREN'T REAL FRIENDS.**

Brian nodded. "I guess not."

**BUT YOU STILL WANT TO WIN
THE REST OF THEIR STUFF FROM
THEM, DON'T YOU?**

"Well . . . I guess so. But they won't bet with me either. No one will."

WE CAN FIX THAT.

"What do you mean?"

THE SUPER BOWL IS NEXT WEEK.

"Sure, I know."

IT'S THE BIGGEST GAME OF THE YEAR.

"So?"

I KNOW HOW TO GET THEM TO BET WITH YOU. AND THEY'LL BE HAPPY ABOUT IT TOO.

"Really? How's that?"

I'LL SHOW YOU. BUT FIRST, DO YOU REMEMBER WE TALKED ABOUT A PRICE?

"A price?"

FOR THE GAME. YOU SAID YOU'D PAY ME AT THE NEXT FLEA MARKET.

"Oh, sure—I remember."

I'LL SHOW YOU HOW TO WIN EVERYTHING FROM YOUR EX FRIENDS. AND FROM AS MANY OTHER PEOPLE AS YOU WANT.

"Okay . . ."

AND IN RETURN

Brian waited. "Yeah?"

Then it came.

YOU AGREE TO GIVE ME A PIECE OF YOUR SOUL.

A chill went through him like a cold breeze. "My . . . my soul?"

THAT'S RIGHT.

"Umm . . . I don't know about that."

NOT ALL OF IT... JUST A LITTLE PIECE. A TINY PIECE.

"I don't understand. How would I do that?"

WE CAN TALK ABOUT THAT WHEN WE SEE EACH OTHER. THE FOOTBALL SEASON WILL BE OVER BY THEN. I'D LIKE TO TALK ABOUT SOME OTHER THINGS TOO. BUT FOR NOW, DO WE HAVE A DEAL?

Brian thought this over a few more times.
He was having trouble making sense of it.

YOU'LL HAVE THE BIGGEST COLLECTION IN THE WORLD, BRIAN. YOU'LL HAVE EVERYTHING.

"Everything?"

EVERYTHING. YOU HAVE MY WORD ON THAT. HAVEN'T I KEPT ALL MY PROMISES?

"Well . . . yes."

OKAY THEN. DO WE HAVE A DEAL?

He looked back at the photo on the dresser.
His sadness came back. But then anger pushed it

away again.

He turned back to the screen with a terrible smile on his face.

"Okay, let's do this," he said. Then he hit the "Y" key with his finger.

EXCELLENT, BRIAN. YOU'VE MADE THE RIGHT CHOICE.

"I'm sure I have."

WELCOME BACK TO ULTIMATE FOOTBALL!

The screen went blank. And then, like always, there was the roar of a huge crowd. After that, the picture of a stadium slowly came onto the screen . . .

Brian's five ex-friends were having lunch in the cafeteria. Then all their phones went off at the same time.

Cameron looked at the screen. He always kept his phone on the table when he ate.

"Brian again. He never knows when to give up."

Lucas and Oliver put their phones back into their pockets. They never even read the message. But Emma did.

"Umm, you might want to see this," she said.

Cameron said, "Not interested."

Lucas said, "Forget it."

Oliver asked, "What for?"

"No kidding, you guys should look," Emma said.

"Okay, fine . . ."

A moment later, Lucas said, "He can't be serious."

Oliver was shaking his head. "How can he expect this to work?"

Emma shrugged. "I have no clue. But how can we turn it down?"

They all looked to Cameron.

"We can't," he said. "This is one bet we have to take."

Walking home later on, they met up with Elijah.

He agreed that the bet was a good idea.

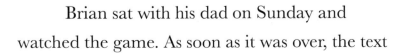

Brian sat with his dad on Sunday and watched the game. As soon as it was over, the text messages started coming in.

"What's all that about, Bri?" his dad asked.

Brian thought for a moment. Then he smiled and said, "Justice."

April

Spring came early to Kennisek. There were record-breaking temperatures on six different days.

The flea market was held on the Saturday at the start of spring break. It was a blue and sunny afternoon. Everyone was in a great mood. Old Mr. Hollister washed the fire trucks until they shined. And Alice Garrett handed out free cups of lemonade.

Brian saw Odium in the far corner of the parking lot again. He had his rusty station wagon. And there were the same piles of computer junk on the table.

As soon as Odium saw Brian coming, his

wrinkly old face lit up with joy.

"Well, if it isn't my young gaming pro. So good to see you!"

Brian smiled. "Thank you."

"After talking to you so much through your computer, I feel like I know you better than ever."

"Yeah, me too. I feel I know you really well now."

Odium pointed to the plastic bag Brian was carrying. "You have been doing some shopping?"

"A little," Brian told him. "Some flower seeds for my mom because she loves gardening. And an old pen for my dad. He collects those."

"How kind of you."

"Thanks."

Odium smiled again. "So, are you happy with the outcome of the last game? The world-famous Super Bowl?"

Brian nodded. "I am. I really am."

"Excellent! And what about those terrible kids who said they were your friends? How did *they* feel about it? Do tell me."

"Just like I thought they would, Mr. Odium. Just like I thought they would."

The old man clapped his hands together. Then he leaned back and laughed.

"How excellent! I am so proud of you, young man!"

"Thanks, I'm proud of me, too."

"Wonderful. So let us get to business. You know about our deal. Are you ready to make it official? Make it *forever*, you might say?"

"I believe I am."

"Good, then all I need now is a simple handshake."

"To seal the deal."

Odium reached across the table. His hand was just as Brian remembered—long and bony.

Every bit like a mummy as those yellow teeth.

Odium closed his eyes. His awful smile grew even wider.

"Go ahead, Brian," he said. "I'm waiting."

"Sure thing," Brian told him. "Here it comes."

"Yes . . ." Odium became very excited now. "*Yes!* Give me some of your soul. Then you will always belong to—"

He stopped suddenly. His eyes opened again. Then he looked down at what Brian had given him.

It was the *Ultimate Football* CD.

"What is this?"

"It's your game," Brian said.

"I don't understand."

"I'm returning it."

"You cannot do that!" Odium said sharply.

"Of course I can. You said yourself I had

it as a kind of 'test period' to see if I liked it. Well, I've tried it out, and I don't."

Odium's face went all crazy. It was like he couldn't decide whether he was confused or angry.

"Well . . . what . . . how . . . no! My program cannot be returned! How do I know you don't still have it on your machine at home?"

Brian laughed. "You know it's still on there. You know very well it can't be taken off. Even if I had tried to erase the files 100%, I couldn't. Don't pretend you don't know that."

"How dare you . . ."

Brian reached into the plastic bag and brought out something else. It was about the size of a small book.

"Here's the hard drive, too," he said. "I already moved off all my important stuff. So here—" He tossed it onto the table with all the other junk. "All yours."

Odium looked like he was about to explode.

"*No one* doesn't want my games!" he growled. "*Everyone wants them! EVERYONE!*"

Brian shook his head. "No, I don't think that's true. I'm sure a few people bring them back. Not many, but a few. I'll bet that's where you got all this other stuff, too. It's probably got your nasty stuff all through it. Black magic or whatever it is. Am I right?"

Odium said nothing, but he looked like he could kill.

"Well *I* don't want it," Brian said. "I thought I did. But it turns out I was just being stupid. And when I realized that, I wanted to get my friends back. So I did. And you know how? I made a *bet* with them. The best bet I ever made. I bet them that they could have all their stuff back if I lost. And if I won, they could *still* have all their stuff back."

"That's not what I told you to do!" Odium said.

"Yeah, but it's what *I* told me to do," Brian shot back. "And that's because I knew there was one more bet here. You were betting that you'd get *me*. That you'd get my soul. Well, sorry to give you the bad news, but you lost that one." He smiled. "And you lost *HUUUGE*."

Odium's face sort of faded away. Then the real creature that lay beneath him was there. It was the most horrible thing Brian had ever seen. Some kind of crazy beast from another world. It had orange-red eyes that glowed with hatred and madness. The skin was ragged and bleeding. And its teeth were dirtier than the mummy teeth. The pointed tips were worn down from whatever poor things it had eaten over the years. Maybe even centuries.

Brian took a step back. The beast-thing's

mouth began to curve into a smile. Then Brian remembered what Elijah had told him earlier that day. *It only has as much power over you as you give it.*

Brian's fear went out of him, and he stepped forward again. Then the creature's face faded, and the old man's came back.

"See you around," Brian said. "*Or not.*"

He turned and walked away.

Elijah was waiting for him at the tables. They put their arms around each other and got lost in the crowd.

Odium watched all this with nothing but hate in his eyes. He picked up Brian's hard drive and threw it on the ground. Then he reached into his car and found a hammer.

I'll pound that thing into a million pieces, he thought. *A million tiny—*

"Excuse me?"

Odium turned and found a boy standing there. He looked maybe twelve or thirteen years old. He had red hair and about a million freckles.

"Yes?"

"I'm looking for old computer programs," the boy said. "I really love the old stuff."

The smile came back to Odium's face right away.

"Then you have come to the right place, my young friend," he said cheerfully.

The boy rubbed his hands together. "Okay, awesome!"

"Yes," the old man said. "Awesome indeed."

Want to Keep Reading?

Turn the page for a sneak peek at
the next book in the series.

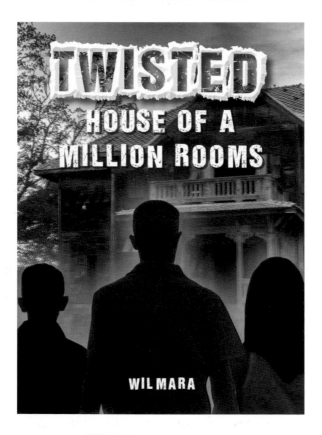

ISBN: 9781538383636

"Wow," Ryan whispered, "it's really there."

"I...I can't believe it," Samantha added.

"It's *so* cool," Josh said excitedly.

They stood along the edge of the forest. There was a long, open field in front of them. And in the middle of the field was a house. It was very old and very big. There was no paint on the outside. Just bare wood that had turned gray from years in the sun. Other than that, it looked to be in good shape. An old house, but a *strong* house.

They couldn't take their eyes off it. They just stood there getting soaked as the rain drove through the trees. It sounded like popcorn in the microwave.

"It's really been here all this time?" Samantha asked. Her long, dark hair was stuck to the sides of her face.

Ryan shrugged. He was the smallest of the three. He was also the only one who wore glasses. "I guess so," he said. "The note was from 1953."

Ryan found the note in an old book. He had been in the school library earlier that day. He was working on a report about colonial America. The library had six different books on the subject. Most of them were pretty new. One, however, looked like it was about to fall apart. Ryan loved books. Sure the Internet was great. But there was nothing like a real book.

He took the old one off the shelf. The first thing he did was open it up and smell it. *Old books have the greatest smell in the world*, he thought. Then he started going through the pages. The pictures were all black and white. And they were drawings, not photographs. Ryan didn't think a book this old could help with the report. But he liked looking through it anyway.

Somewhere around the middle, he found a folded sheet of paper. It was caught between two pages. When he unfolded it, he saw writing from top to bottom. The ink wasn't black anymore. It had turned brown over time. Then he noticed the date at the top—June 7, 1953. *Wow*, he thought. *It's been here THAT long...*

There were two different types of handwriting. He read the first few lines—

Are you going to Alan's party on Saturday?

　　I'm not sure. My mom and dad probably won't let me.
　　Are you?

Yeah.

　　It sounds like it'll be swell.

It will be! You just have to go!

This was some kind of a secret note, he realized. Someone left it in a book. Then another person found it and wrote a reply. It went back and forth like that until whenever. *Today we just send text messages*, Ryan thought. *But they didn't have cell phones in 1953.*

He was pretty sure it was between a boy and a girl. The boy really wanted the girl to go to this party. He kept asking, and she kept giving reasons why she couldn't. *Bo-ring!* Ryan thought.

Then he turned the note over. There was more writing on the other side. At first it was just the same stuff. Then it wasn't so boring after all. In fact, it was anything *but*—

Me and Greg are going to check out that old house.
  What old house?
The one out on the west side of town. Through the woods.

You know you can't do that!

Why not?

Carl, that place is bad news. And if you get caught, you'll be in SO much trouble!

I hear it's haunted! Who wouldn't want to check out a house that's haunted? It'll be a blast!

It doesn't matter! You know no one is allowed to go near it! NOBODY!

That's what my mom said when I asked her about it.

My parents have told me over and over never to go near it! They bug me about it at least once a year! One time I asked them why, and they grounded me for a week!

My mom told me never to ask about it again. Boy, was she mad!

Carl, PLEASE promise me you won't go near it! PLEASE???

Will you go to Alan's with me on Saturday?

Yes, yes, I'll figure something out. But please promise me!

Okay, I promise.

Ryan showed Josh the note. Then Josh showed Samantha. A few hours later, here they were.

ABOUT THE AUTHOR

Wil Mara has been an author for over 30 years and has more than 200 books to his credit. His work for children includes more than 150 educational titles for the school and library markets, and he has also ghostwritten five of the popular Boxcar Children mysteries. His 2013 thriller *Frame 232* reached the #1 spot in its category on Amazon and won the Lime Award for Excellence in Fiction. He is also an associate member of the NJASL, and an executive member of the Board of Directors for the New Jersey Center for the Book, an affiliate of the US Library of Congress. He lives with his family in New Jersey.

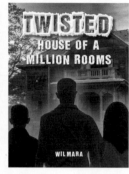

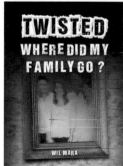
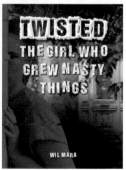